A Prayer for Mother

Alice, An Adventist Girl

~ BOOK FOUR ~

SANDY ZAUGG

Pacific Press® Publishing Association
Nampa, Idaho
Oshawa, Ontario, Canada
www.pacificpress.com

Edited by Elizabeth Lechleitner
Designed by Dennis Ferree
Cover and inside illustrations by Matthew Archambault
Research for cover illustration provided by
Judy M. Johnson

Copyright © 2005 by
Pacific Press® Publishing Association
Printed in the United States of America
All Rights Reserved

Additional copies of this book are available by
calling toll free 1-800-765-6955
or visiting http://www.adventistbookcenter.com

Library of Congress Cataloging-in-Publication Data

Zaugg, Sandra L., 1938-
A prayer for mother / Sandy Zaugg.
p. cm. — (Alice, an Adventist girl; bk 4)
Summary: In 1927, Alice is comfortably settled in China,
helping with her parents' missionary work, when her
mother becomes sick with tuberculosis and Alice, aided by
some surprise visitors, learns to trust God's will.
ISBN: 0-8163-2056-X
[1. Tuberculosis. 2. Sick. 3. Missionaries.
4.Seventh-day Adventists. 5. Shanghai (China)
6. China—History—1912-1928.]
I. Title.

PZ7.Z2675Pr 2005

dc22   2004057335

05 06 07 08 09 • 5 4 3 2 1

Dedication

To Catherine Zhong, my young
Chinese friend, who spent many
hours showing me Shanghai
and the two hospitals
Dr. Miller built there.—sz

Contents

CHAPTER 1

Questions

"Well, my dear, here we go again!" Mother said when they were settled on the rickshaw's narrow wooden bench. The man hired to pull them, called a "coolie," picked up the poles and began jogging down the busy street.

"I wonder how many will come to this class," Alice said.

"Let's see, this is the fourth time we've taught this series of classes, isn't it?" Mother said. "The fourth time you've given Sally a bath in front of a group of women."

"She's the cleanest doll in China!" Alice laughed and patted the bag in her lap. "And she's all ready for another bath. Mother, what do we do when we run out of people to teach?"

"If it's safe enough, we could teach these classes on the other side of the city, I suppose." Mother's forehead wrinkled as she continued. "Daddy and Dr. Miller want me to develop a class for expectant mothers. They say Chinese mothers don't eat the right foods to produce healthy babies. But I don't think they would listen, since I have only two children and many of them have eight or ten." Mother cleared her throat. "They would just laugh and say I don't know anything about it."

Questions

As they bumped along in the rickshaw, Alice watched a man walking along the street with a pole across his shoulders. Piles of bricks were stacked on small platforms that hung from each end of the pole. From the way he struggled, she could tell the bricks were very heavy. She watched him dodge a dog fight, then wait for a group of noisy schoolboys to pass.

The coolie pulled the rickshaw down a narrow lane lined with shops. Then he slowed down for the sharp turn through the iron gates to the new hospital. Alice loved to look at the tall white pillars that held up the round porch roof. The outside of the hospital looked finished. But Daddy had explained that since there was still plenty to finish on the inside, the hospital wasn't open for business yet. And he couldn't perform any operations until it was.

On the hospital grounds, Alice saw her friend Mr. Cheng standing in front of the building. He held a large paper in his hand. He was looking from the paper to the building and back again. When he noticed Alice, he waved and walked over to greet her.

"Hello, Missy Alice," he greeted. Then he bowed to Mother. "Madam Stewart, it is honorable to see you. I hear much good reports about the classes you and the little missy be teaching."

Mother laughed and shook his hand. "It's good to see you, Mr. Cheng. Are you still enjoying your job here?"

"I cannot tell you my appreciation for this position," he said. His face beamed. "I now attempt more to learn about building. I hold here the drawings for this work, and I now try to see how it goes together."

They said Goodbye to Mr. Cheng and went in to prepare for their class. During the class, Alice noticed that Mother coughed several times while she was talking.

Hmmm, Alice thought, *I guess I'd better remember to bring some water for Mother next time. Her voice must get tired from talking so much.*

When they returned home, they found that a box had arrived from Grandma and Grandpa. Inside was a small package for Alice.

"It's a book! I know it is!" She ripped off the paper and read the title out loud. "*Ann of Green Gables.* Oh, Mother, look!" she exclaimed, holding up the book. "Isn't Grandma nice? I've heard about this book, but I've never read it."

A PRAYER FOR MOTHER

Mother admired the book with her. "Don't forget to write and thank her." She looked at the outside of the box and smiled. "My, it's taken three months to get here! By now, Grandma may have forgotten she sent it."

Alice spent the next hour curled up on her bed reading. A soft breeze flowed in through the open door. Outside, she could see her little brother, Johnny, playing with a tiny wooden boat. He floated it down a small ditch of dirty water along the back wall.

"Al Lees!" called a voice from outside. "Al Lees!"

"I'm coming, Li Li!" she called. She slipped her new book under her pillow and went out into the courtyard. Looking up, she spotted her friend on the roof. "Can you come over and play?" Alice asked in Chinese.

Questions

"OK," Li Li answered in English. She scrambled out of sight. A few minutes later she clanged the bell at the outside door. Soon they had all of Sally's clothes spread out on the bed. Most of their words were spoken in Chinese. Li Li helped Alice with words she got stuck on. And each time they played, Li Li learned some new English words.

Alice wanted to share her new book with her friend, but she knew Li Li didn't know enough English to understand the story. And Alice didn't know enough Chinese to explain it. When they tired of playing with Sally, they sat on the bed and talked for a while.

"Al Lees, when are you going to have another Sabbath School?" Li Li asked. "You haven't had one for a long time. I could help you, couldn't I?"

A PRAYER FOR MOTHER

Alice grinned. "That would be fun! Let's plan one! I'll get a piece of paper and we can write down ideas. Mother says that's the best way to do it."

She bounded off the bed and returned a few moments later waving a paper and pencil. "Now, what's your favorite Bible story?"

Li Li bounced up and down. "I know! I like the story about Jesus. You know, when He built that big boat and got all the animals to go inside."

Alice laughed. "That was Noah! I guess I'll have to tell you that story again. Jesus was the One nailed up on the cross."

"Those must have been wicked men to do that—as wicked as the Green Gang. I heard my father telling my mother that the Green Gang killed four people in Shanghai last weekend."

Questions

Alice shivered. "Let's talk about our Sabbath School," she said. "I like that better."

Together they made a list of stories and songs they could use.

"We need to do something else," Alice said. "At the end of Sabbath School, I always give everyone something to take home, remember? We'll have to make something to give them this time."

Both girls thought for a few minutes.

"It'll have to be something simple and quick to make," Alice said. "Lots of kids came last time."

Li Li grinned. "I counted thirty-one!"

"I've got an idea!" Alice exclaimed. "What if we tell them about heaven? About how Jesus will come to take us to heaven with Him. And we could make paper crowns for everybody!"

"I'd like that." Then Li Li looked silently at Alice for a moment. Finally, she said, "Do you really know that Jesus will come back to take people to heaven?"

"Oh, yes! The Bible says so."

"Really?"

Alice scooted off the bed and pulled her little Bible off a nearby shelf. She turned its pages, looking for a memory verse she knew.

She opened her Bible to John 14. "Here it is." Then she stopped. Her Bible was in English and she needed to read to Li Li in Chinese. She sent up a quick prayer. *Help me do this, Jesus.*

"Um, it says here that Jesus went to heaven to fix up places for us to live. When He's finished, He'll come get the people who love Him and take them back to heaven to live forever."

Questions

Li Li looked at her hands. Then she raised her head. "What will heaven be like?"

"It will be wonderful!" Alice exclaimed. "Nobody will get hurt; nobody will be mean. The animals will be tame. The flowers will always bloom. And we'll get to see Jesus!"

"No Green Gang to kill people?" Li Li asked. "No murders or grandmas with bound feet?"

Alice nodded. "We won't have to be afraid of anything. And we'll live forever."

"It *does* sound wonderful." Li Li said. Then she heard her mother call, so she scooted off the bed. "I need to go home now. Will you tell me more about heaven next time?"

"Sure I will. And don't forget, we have a lot of crowns to make and stories to learn. So come back tomorrow if you can, OK?"

When Alice went to bed that night, she didn't go right to sleep. She had a lot of thinking to do. No one had ever asked her questions about Jesus or heaven before.

Dear Jesus, did I do OK today? she prayed. *I think I'm going to need Your help a lot now when Li Li's around. Will she want to be one of Your special children?*

Finally, Alice snuggled down under her blanket. She drifted off to sleep, thinking about tame lions and raccoons she could hold. In her dreams, she and Li Li were walking by a river, each holding Jesus' hand. A big blue parrot flew down and landed on her shoulder.

During the middle of the night, a muffled sound woke Alice up. She sat up in bed and looked around in the

Questions

darkness. Was something in her room? Then she heard it again. Someone was coughing. And coughing. And coughing. Mother? Why did Mother suddenly cough so much? *Maybe she's getting a cold,* Alice thought. She heard footsteps cross the courtyard. Then she heard Daddy's voice. "Here, Millie, drink this water," he said. Mother's answer faded away as Alice slipped back into her dream about heaven.

CHAPTER 2

What
About
Mother?

Alice's favorite room in the whole house was the new library. Grandpa had shipped Daddy's books to China. And Daddy had shelves made for them in the room between Alice's room and the living room. The library also had a small desk and chair left by the former owner. Mother bought some big, brightly colored pillows to cushion the wooden floor. Alice loved to curl up on the pillows and read. She pretended she was back in the cozy library they'd had at home in Portland. There, bookshelves had covered three walls, and a big globe had stood on the thick carpet.

But in this library, only three shelves ran along one wall. Long narrow Chinese paintings of mountain scenes hung on the other walls. A ceiling fan whirred gently overhead. In one corner, a box held white paper, colored paper, crayons, scissors, and glue.

Alice rummaged through the box and found several sheets of yellow paper. She put the paper on the desk and found a pencil. Using scratch paper, she tried to draw a crown. After she cut it out, she made a face. The crown was so lopsided that she laughed out loud and went to find Mother. She heard coughing coming from the dining room. She found Mother there with Poh-Poh, planning the next shopping trip.

"Mother, I want to make crowns for my next Sabbath School." Alice held up her strange-looking creation. "But this looks like it slid off the table and crashed." Mother and Poh-Poh smiled.

"Bring me a piece of scratch paper and the scissors and I'll see what I can do," Mother offered.

When Alice brought them, Mother folded the paper in half and began to cut at the top of the fold. To Alice, it looked like she cut half a big mountain and then some little peaks. When she unfolded it, there was a big point in the center.

"That's good, Mother!" Alice exclaimed. "But it won't fit around anybody's head, will it?"

What About Mother?

"Not like this. You'll have to take another piece of paper and cut a long strip, the same height as the outside edges of this crown. Glue the strip to one side of the crown. Then, when the children come, you can just fasten the other side to fit each child."

"But how will I fasten it? Glue will take too long to dry, and I want them to wear the crowns during Sabbath School," Alice said.

"Ask Daddy if you can use some of his paper clips. I know he brought some boxes of them from home."

Alice clapped her hands together. "Oh, Mother! That will be perfect! I'll ask him as soon as he comes home tonight." Alice lingered by the door a moment before she went out. "Um, Mother?" she began. "Mother, you're sure coughing a lot. Are you catching a cold?"

"I don't think so," Mother replied. "I'm probably just allergic to something in the air. I'll be fine again soon. Don't you worry about me."

Mother didn't seem fine to Alice. Slowly she went back to the library, thinking about Mother. But she busied herself tracing crowns on yellow paper and soon forgot all about Mother's coughing. *If Li Li comes over later,* she thought, *we can cut the crowns out together and maybe use crayons to make colored jewels on each one.*

Li Li did come, and the girls cut out and decorated many crowns. Alice taught Li Li another song about Jesus. By the end of the afternoon, both girls were satisfied with their plans for Sabbath School the next week.

Daddy gave permission to use the paper clips, but he added, "Be sure not

What About Mother?

to waste any, Little Lady. We can't buy any more in China, so when these are gone, we won't have any."

During supper, Alice noticed Daddy watching Mother nibble at her food. His eyebrows pulled together like they did when he was worried. When Mother noticed him, she smiled, sat up straighter, and began talking about Johnny's latest words.

Later that evening, after Alice had gone to bed, she heard Daddy pause outside her door. "I'm still awake, Daddy," she called. "I'm just reading."

Daddy came in and sat down on the edge of her bed. He still looked worried.

"Daddy, is Mother getting sick?"

"What makes you ask that?" he asked.

"Well, she coughs so much," Alice replied. "She's never coughed like she does now. She told me it's just an allergy. But—is she sick?"

"So, she coughs a lot during the day, too?"

"Uh-huh." Alice nodded her head. "More every day."

Daddy stroked his chin and looked at the wall like he was thinking. "I think we'd better watch Mother," he said. "She says nothing is wrong, but I'm not so sure. I think she just doesn't want us to worry."

"What can we do, Daddy?"

"Right now, there's not much we can do, except ask Jesus to keep her well. And we'll help her all we can." He kissed Alice's forehead. "Good night, Little Lady. Dream about running through heaven with a crown on your head!"

What About Mother?

After Daddy left, Alice lay for a long time, listening to the night sounds. She could still hear people going by in the street. And she could even tell what they were shouting. A year ago, she couldn't understand anything in Chinese. But now, she often understood what people were saying. In the dark, she smiled.

Earlier in the day, she had received two letters from her best friend Ruth in America. Ruth told her all about what was happening at her old school in Portland. Tomorrow, when she returned from her classes at the Millers' house, she'd write to Ruth. She'd tell her about the Sabbath School she and Li Li were planning and about the new hospital that was going to be finished soon.

Thank You, Jesus, she prayed, *for Li Li here and Ruth at home. But I wish Ruth could visit me. Li Li and I would have such fun with her. She could help us plan a Sabbath School. And I'm sure Mr. Cheng would come and take us to see things in the city.*

And, Jesus, what about Mother? Is she getting sick? Help her not to cough so much. Even right now I can hear her. It sounds scary, doesn't it? Please make her stop coughing.

CHAPTER 3

"Please, Dear Jesus"

Thirty-six neighborhood children came to the Sabbath School the girls planned. Johnny sat near the front with the younger children. He proudly wore the yellow crown he had decorated himself the day before. Mr. Cheng came with his nieces and nephews. They were among the first to arrive. He soon took over the job of fitting the crowns on the heads of the children. Then he sat behind the children and smiled and sang and listened to the stories just like they did.

On the way out, several children bowed to Alice and said, "I want to go to heaven, too."

When almost all the children had gone home, Mr. Cheng helped the girls fold up the mats the children sat on. Before he said Goodbye, he reached into a hidden pocket in his long skirt and brought out a small package wrapped in newspaper and tied with string. It was about the size of a man's shoe. He held it out to Alice with both hands and bowed as he gave it to her.

"This is a poor gift to be presenting to your honored self," he said. "But I hope you will accept it. My number three sister made it for you."

"Please, Dear Jesus"

Alice reached out and took the gift with both hands, as she had been taught to do in China. She tried be serious, but her smile peeked through.

"Oh, Mr. Cheng!" she exclaimed. "Thank you so much. I know I'll love it." She hugged the package to her chest. She could hardly wait to open it, but Poh-Poh had taught her well: accept a gift with two hands and don't open it in front of the giver.

"I notice today that Madam Stewart is not present," Mr. Cheng said. "Is she well?"

"She said she was a little tired," Alice answered. "She went to rest on her bed."

Li Li was the last one to go home. Alice was finally free to open her present. She went to the kitchen, where

Poh-Poh was preparing the evening meal.

"Look, Poh-Poh!" she said, holding up the package. "Mr. Cheng gave me a present."

Carefully, she untied the string and unwrapped the newspaper and then some white paper underneath. Then she stared in amazement. "Oh, look, Poh-Poh," she gasped. "It's beautiful!"

Alice held up a pale blue shirt with a high collar and long sleeves. Mr. Cheng's third sister had decorated the front of it with vines and flowers embroidered in pink, red, and gold thread. Alice slipped it on and tried to see what it looked like.

"I'll go look in Mother's mirror," she said. As she turned to go, Poh-Poh stopped her.

"Please, Dear Jesus"

"Wait," Poh-Poh said, holding her finger to her lips. "Don't wake up madam," she said.

Alice stepped into the courtyard where Johnny was playing—still wearing his crown. She thought back to when she first came to China and couldn't talk to Poh-Poh or Li Li. Now they could visit just fine. True, she didn't know all the Chinese words she heard, but she knew enough to understand and talk to most people. That made life a lot more fun.

Mother's door was open, so she looked in. Mother lay on her bed holding a book, but not reading.

"Are you OK, Mother?" Alice asked.

"Of course, my dear," Mother said as she sat up. "What a beautiful shirt! Where did you get it?"

"Mr. Cheng gave it to me. He came

to Sabbath School." Alice twirled around. "I think it's pretty, too."

Mother smiled, coughing a little. Alice examined her new shirt in the mirror.

"Mother, are you sure you're not sick?" Alice asked as she turned away from the mirror. "You never used to take naps during the day. And you're getting really skinny."

Mother started to laugh, but then began coughing. When she caught her breath again, she shrugged her shoulders. "I'm not sure what's happening to me. If it was just a cold, it should have gone away by now. But it seems to be getting worse. I guess I'd better talk to Daddy about it." She stood up. "But don't worry. It's probably nothing." She put her arm around Alice. "Why don't you leave your new shirt on until after supper. It really is lovely."

At supper, Mother picked at her food. "It's delicious," she told Poh-Poh. "I'm just not very hungry right now."

After supper, Mother said she was tired and went to her room. Alice finally said what was on her mind.

"Daddy, Mother's not well, is she? She stayed in bed all afternoon. And when I went in, she couldn't stop coughing for a while."

Daddy's forehead scrunched up and his eyebrows pulled together. "I'm worried too. I plan to take her to see Dr. Miller tomorrow. He knows a lot about sicknesses people get here in China." Daddy stood up. "I forgot to tell Mother about that. Guess I'd better go do it."

A PRAYER FOR MOTHER

Half an hour later, he came back. He looked even more worried. For a few minutes, he sat without speaking.

Alice was afraid. She sat quietly looking at Daddy, waiting to see what he would say. After what seemed like a long time, he ran his hand through his hair and looked at Alice. "I think we'd better move Johnny's bed into your room tonight," he said.

Alice opened her mouth to object, but Daddy held up his hand. "I know you're not excited about it, but I think it's best." He got up. "In fact, come on. Let's go do it right now."

Alice still wanted to grumble, but something on Daddy's face made her keep quiet. Mother lay on the bed and watched silently as they opened the door between the two bedrooms. Together they pushed the crib and the

"Please, Dear Jesus"

chest with Johnny's clothes into Alice's room. Then Alice helped put Johnny to bed. He thought it was great fun to be in her room. He giggled as he made faces at Alice through the slats of his crib.

"Good night, Johnny," Daddy said, patting his cheek. Then he took Alice by the hand and led her out of the room. "Let's see if we can catch Poh-Poh before she goes home. I'll need your help. Your Chinese is better than mine."

Together they explained to Poh-Poh what she already knew—that Mother was sick. Daddy asked if Poh-Poh could spend more time with them to care for Johnny and Alice. Then Poh-Poh started talking fast. She waved her hands in the air, she pointed toward the living room, she even copied Mother's cough.

A PRAYER FOR MOTHER

When she stopped and looked at Daddy with her eyebrows raised, he looked completely puzzled. He turned to Alice.

"What was all that about?" he asked.

"As near as I can understand, Poh-Poh says Mother's been getting sick for several weeks. She is offering to come here to stay while Mother is sick. She says she can sleep in the living room, and we can use the library for a sitting room."

Daddy smiled. He turned to Poh-Poh and bowed. In simple Chinese, he said, "Thank you, thank you. I am so thankful for your help. Please, can you begin living here tomorrow?"

"Certainly," Poh-Poh said. "I shall not let harm come to your little ones."

Some of the wrinkles in Daddy's forehead smoothed out. Later, when

"Please, Dear Jesus"

Daddy and Alice were alone, Daddy talked to her like she was a grown-up. That made her feel important. Daddy said he needed her to be very helpful while Mother was sick. Being more grown up meant she'd have more responsibility and more work. Alice wasn't sure she'd like that.

"Alice," Daddy said, "besides her coughing, Mother is running a fever. She's not eating enough to keep a hummingbird alive, and she's very tired all the time. I don't like the sound of it. Tomorrow we'll see Dr. Miller. I hope he tells me I'm wrong, and that Mother's not seriously sick." He took Alice's hand. "There's a chance we might need to take Mother home to America."

Alice opened her mouth, but shut it again. Mother's health was more important than her next Sabbath School or the spelling test next week.

"What's wrong with her?" Alice asked.

Daddy stroked his chin and spoke slowly, like he was thinking to himself. "Have you ever heard of tuberculosis?"

"No—what's that?"

"Sometimes, it's just called TB," he added.

"Oh, yes! A while back Mother took some food to a family who had TB," she said. "I remember because she wouldn't let me go with her."

"So that explains it." Daddy sat back. "TB is very contagious—that means it's easy to pass from one person to another. That's why I moved Johnny out of our room. I should have done it last week." Then he turned to Alice and looked straight at her. "I want you and Johnny

"Please, Dear Jesus"

to keep away from Mother. Spend as much time outdoors as you can. Be sure to wash your hands often. And wash Johnny's hands too."

"What about you, Daddy? Won't you get TB too?"

"I'm going to make a bed for myself in the library. I'll still have to care for Mother, but I'll be very careful about germs."

"What about the classes at the hospital?"

"I'll get Mr. Cheng to pass the word that they won't be continued."

"Daddy?" Alice paused to blink back tears. But she had to ask. "Daddy, is Mother going to die?"

Daddy ran his hands through his hair again and rubbed his eyes. "Pray, Alice. Pray like you've never prayed before. We need Mother." He swallowed hard before he went on. "This is 1927. Times have changed, and medicine has advanced. But we still can't do much about TB. If Mother gets lots of rest and good care and a lot of help from the Lord, she'll pull through."

He got up and paced the length of the room and back. "If only I could get her home to an American hospital."

Alice and Daddy talked together for a long time that night. Alice had never really thought about her parents before. They were, well, her parents. But now she saw them differently. She saw how much Daddy loved Mother and how worried he was about her.

Later, she knelt beside her bed for her nightly talk with Jesus.

Oh, dear Jesus, please help Mother. I don't want her to die. Johnny needs her. And

"Please, Dear Jesus"

so do Daddy and I. Mother is so good, Jesus. She was just helping out some sick people, and now she's really sick. Please make her well. Please!

For a long time that night, Alice lay in her bed and stared into the darkness. Johnny rolled over in his sleep and hit the side of his bed. Mother coughed. Sometimes she heard carts rumble by in the street. A tear slid down her cheek. Then another. And another . . . until she couldn't stop them. She cried herself to sleep.

CHAPTER 4

Sad Times

"Al-lie!" Johnny sang, as he looked through the slats of his bed. "Allie, Allie."

Alice rolled over and groaned, remembering she now shared her room with her baby brother.

"What do you want?" she said sleepily.

"Up, Allie, up." He held up his arms. "Help me—up!" She knew he couldn't

Sad Times

get out of his crib by himself. The sides were too high.

"OK, I give up," she said as she rolled out of bed. She helped Johnny climb out. Then she got dressed quickly and went to find Poh-Poh. Daddy gave her a crooked smile as he passed to go check on Mother.

Suddenly, Alice heard a shriek and a giggle. She whirled around. Johnny was running around the courtyard, waving his arms. He was wearing absolutely nothing! His pajamas lay on the concrete near the bedroom door.

"Johnny!" Alice yelled and ran after him. When she caught him, he wiggled free and took off again. From the kitchen door, Poh-Poh called him. He ran over to her, and she picked him up. At that moment, Mother stepped out of her bedroom. Daddy was right behind her.

A PRAYER FOR MOTHER

"Alice, thank you for letting Johnny stay in your . . ." Mother's voice trailed off and she got a funny look on her face. Then her eyes closed, and she slowly sank to the ground. Daddy caught her before her head hit the concrete.

As Alice watched, she felt her lower lip tremble. She was afraid—afraid that Mother might die. Was she dead already? Alice wanted to run to her room and cry. Instead, she opened the bedroom door for Daddy. He carried Mother in and laid her on the bed.

"Don't worry, Little Lady," he said. "Mother's only fainted. And it's no wonder. She's hardly eaten anything for a week or more."

Alice stood beside Daddy as they watched Mother's eyelids flutter, then open wide.

Sad Times

"I'm so sorry," she said in a soft voice. "I don't know what happened to me."

Daddy turned to Alice. "Please ask Poh-Poh to get us a rickshaw right now. I'm taking Mother to see Dr. Miller."

"But you're a doctor, Daddy," Alice argued.

"Dr. Miller knows a lot more than I do about the diseases here," he said.

"But don't people have TB in America?"

"Yes, they do, but I'm a surgeon. I didn't take care of them. Go, Alice. Please!" He nudged her on the back to hurry her out of the room.

About two o'clock that afternoon, Daddy returned. He was alone.

"Where's Mother?" Alice asked.

Daddy reached for her hand and motioned for Poh-Poh to follow. He led them into the library. They all sat down on the floor pillows.

When he spoke, he used simple Chinese words. "I left Mother at the hospital. We put her in one of the finished rooms. We hired some nurses to take care of her. Well, they aren't exactly nurses, but they have experience in caring for the ill." He bowed his head for a moment. His shoulders sagged.

"She does have tuberculosis," he finally said. "And we can't take her home to America. No ship would let her on board now—not with TB."

Johnny stuck his head in the room. "Mama?" he asked. "Where's Mama?"

Daddy reached out for him. "Mama's not here, Johnny. Mama's at the hospital. She's sick."

Johnny's little face puckered up and

Sad Times

tears spilled down his cheeks. "Mama! I want my mama!" he cried.

Poh-Poh took him from Daddy and talked softly to him. Then she carried him out of the room. Daddy ran his hands through his hair and rubbed his face.

"This is going to be tough for all of us, but especially for Johnny. He's too young to understand," Daddy said.

Alice leaned against Daddy. She almost wished she was too young to understand. It all seemed too much for their little family.

"We need Grandma, don't we?" Alice said. "I wish she and Grandpa lived closer."

"Me, too," Daddy said. "But even if I wired them to come, it might take a month for them to find a ship and book passage. Then the ship might not leave for another month. And remember how long we were on the ship?"

Alice nodded.

"But I will send a telegram, so they'll know Mother is sick," Daddy said. "At least that way we'll know they'll be praying for her, too. What we need to do now is to try to go on just like Mother was here. The gardener from the hospital will come as usual to take you to the Millers' place for school each morning. In the afternoons, you can still play with Johnny or Li Li. But I need you to help Poh-Poh as much as you can. I'll try to always be here for supper and worship in the evenings."

"How long will Mother have to stay in the hospital?"

"Until she is well," Daddy said. "It's hard to say how long that will be. TB can spread from one person to another very fast. In America, infected people are sent to special hospitals just for TB cases. That way, the disease won't spread to their families."

"What do they do here?" Alice asked.

Daddy sighed. "Nothing. China is a poor country right now. They have no place to send TB patients, so they stay at home. And lots of times the TB spreads to the rest of their family. It's very sad."

"That's why we came to China, isn't it?" Alice asked. "Because people here need help."

Alice and Daddy talked for a long time that afternoon. Later, he went back to the hospital to check on Mother. When he returned, he and Poh-Poh cleaned the bedroom carefully. They scrubbed the floor and walls and doors—anywhere there might be germs from the TB. They changed the bedding and washed the curtains. Only then did Daddy move his makeshift bed back into his room.

Day followed day. And week followed week. Alice wanted to see Mother so badly that at night she sometimes cried. But she smiled bravely during the day.

Dear Jesus, she prayed one night, *Mother's been gone for a long time. I want her to come home. Johnny cries for her a lot. And I guess I do too. I miss her so much. So does Daddy. Make her well soon. Please, Jesus.*

CHAPTER 5

Unexpected Visitors

One morning when Alice got up, she found Daddy stripping the sheets off his bed. "Daddy, what are you doing that for? Poh-Poh always changes the sheets on Monday, and this is only Thursday."

Daddy turned to her and smiled. He looked happy! He hadn't looked happy since Mother got sick.

"Daddy?" she asked. "What are you so happy about?"

A PRAYER FOR MOTHER

Daddy winked and said, "Oh, you'll find out!"

"Mother's coming home today, isn't she?" Alice squealed and clapped her hands. She even jumped up and down. She was too excited to hold still.

Daddy's smile faded. "No, Little Lady. Mother won't be home for a while yet. But how would you like to go see her?"

Alice jumped up and down again. "Could I? Could I really? I miss her so much. When can I go see her?"

"Soon," Daddy said. "You won't be able to get near her, but you can talk to her from the doorway. So start thinking about something nice to tell her." Daddy smiled again. His eyes sparkled.

"Is that why you're so happy?"

Daddy hugged her. "It's time for you to get ready for school, isn't it?"

Unexpected Visitors

"Daddy?"

"I'm not telling. You'll find out soon."

After school that afternoon, Poh-Poh strapped Johnny to her back, and she and Alice went to the market. Poh-Poh picked out mangos to buy while Alice admired the silk cloth on the next table.

Suddenly, someone screamed and someone else yelled, "Green Gang! Run!"

Poh-Poh dropped the mangos and grabbed Alice's arm. She pulled Alice quickly away from the market. They ran down a narrow side street. Johnny giggled as he bounced on Poh-Poh's back. They didn't stop running until Poh-Poh pushed Alice through a small door. Other shoppers crowded in after them.

When she caught her breath, Alice looked around. They were inside a Buddhist temple. She'd been in one before, and she knew why she was here now. Gangs wouldn't fight in temples, so they were safe places to hide. A shiny, golden Buddha smiled down at her. His fat tummy looked like it would shake if he could laugh. Fresh flowers lay in front of him on a low table. Sweet-smelling incense burned in big pots. The smoke from the incense clouded the room.

Looking into the dark shadows on the left, Alice saw three fierce-looking statues with ugly faces. She shuddered, glad they weren't real.

When the noise outside quieted down, they went back to the market and bought the mangos. They also bought fresh green and yellow vegetables. Alice couldn't remember the names of them, but she knew she liked them. Then they went home.

Unexpected Visitors

Later in the afternoon, Li Li came over to play. Li Li was teaching Alice to write in Chinese. It was hard to make the squiggly little lines and the straight little lines in just the right places to create a word. If she got the squiggles wrong, Li Li would burst into laughter. Then she would tell Alice that she made the character for "woman" instead of "house." Before she left, Li Li asked more questions about Jesus and being a Christian.

After Li Li went home, Alice found Poh-Poh in the dining room. She was setting the table for five people.

"Poh-Poh, are we having company?" she asked. "There are two extra places." Alice knew that Poh-Poh refused to sit and eat with the family. She said it wasn't proper for her to do that. She was hired to serve them.

"Poh-Poh?" Alice said again.

A PRAYER FOR MOTHER

Poh-Poh grinned and shook her head. But she wouldn't answer. She just finished setting the table and went back to preparing the meal.

Finally, Alice shrugged her shoulders and went to her room to read. She started reading *Anne of Green Gables* for the third time. Johnny was "helping" Poh-Poh in the kitchen. Alice's bedroom door stood open so the fresh air could come in. She could hear noises from the street and Poh-Poh talking to Johnny in the kitchen. But she soon lost herself in her book.

But then she heard something that made her throw down the book and spring off her bed.

A big, booming voice called, "Where's my granddaughter?"

"Grandpa? *Grandpa!*" she shrieked. "*Grandma!*" She raced across the con-

Unexpected Visitors

crete and threw herself into Grandpa's arms. Then she ran to Grandma and hugged her. Tears ran down Alice's cheeks—and down Grandma's too. Alice kept going from one to the other while Johnny stared from his safe spot behind them—in Daddy's arms.

Finally Alice hugged Daddy. "Now I know why you were so happy this morning," she said, dancing around. "And I know why Poh-Poh set extra places at the table. What a wonderful surprise!"

Johnny wiggled out of Daddy's arms to look more closely at these strange people. Grandma tried to hug him, but he backed away.

"No!" he protested. "No touch me."

"But I'm your grandma, baby," Grandma said. "I guess you don't remember me."

Johnny shook his little head. "I not baby," he said. "I be a big boy!" Then he said a few words Grandma didn't understand.

"What did he say?" she asked, looking at Daddy.

"He asked if you were going to stay here," Daddy answered with a laugh. "You see, his language is a mix of English and Chinese. It does get confusing sometimes for his listeners." Daddy picked up a suitcase. "Come on, Dad," he said. "Let's get you settled. You're staying in our room. I'll bunk down in the library again. Poh-Poh can move back to her house now, so we'll have the living room free again."

He showed them around the strange little house. "It's a traditional floor plan for a Chinese house," he said.

Grandma objected to the bathroom.

Unexpected Visitors

"I want a toilet I can sit on," she said. "Not just a hole in the floor." But she approved of the rest of the house.

Poh-Poh had prepared a wonderful meal with lots of chopped vegetables. After Grandpa said the blessing for the meal, he picked up his chopsticks and tried to eat. He soon gave up.

"How's a person supposed to survive, eating with sticks?" he demanded. "People should use forks like Christian folks!"

Daddy burst out laughing. "Being a Christian has nothing to do with it, Dad. But being American does." He got up. "I'll get you a fork. How about you, Mom? Want a fork?"

Grandma grinned. "I could stand to lose a little weight, but I think I'll accept that fork instead, thank you."

Before they left the table, Daddy

said, "By the way, Alice, I talked to your teacher yesterday. You may stay home from school tomorrow."

"Oh, goody!" Alice squealed. She jumped up from her chair and ran to give Daddy a hug. "Thank you, thank you!"

"Well," Daddy said, "I'm taking the day off, too. I figured we'd like to stay with Grandma and Grandpa."

He looked around at each of them with a smile. "And," he began importantly, "tomorrow we will go see Mother."

By worship time, Alice felt a warm glow in her heart. It had been a happy evening—just like before Mother got sick. Well, almost.

At bedtime, Grandma tucked Alice in and kissed her, just like Mother did. Johnny was already asleep in his crib. Alice could hear his quiet, steady breathing.

Unexpected Visitors

"I'm so glad you came," Alice said, hanging on to Grandma's hand.

Grandma sat down on the edge of her bed. "I'm glad I came too."

"If only Mother were well, everything would be perfect."

"Well, my dear," Grandma said, looking sad, "your mother is very sick. When your daddy wired us, I knew we had to come. And the Lord worked a miracle. We were able to get on a ship within a week. Your mother is very special to me. She is special to Jesus, too, remember. If it's His will, He'll make her well." Then she kissed Alice again and left the room.

His will? What does Grandma mean? Alice wondered. *Of course Jesus wants Mother to get well—doesn't He? . . . Doesn't He?*

CHAPTER 6

Lots
of
Prayers

At breakfast the next morning, Grandpa looked at the chopped vegetables and rice on the table. He looked at Daddy and Alice, then back at his plate.

"Where's the oatmeal?" he demanded.

"Welcome to China, Dad," Daddy said. "This is what we eat."

"Until now," Grandpa said, "I didn't realize how hard mission life is."

Lots of Prayers

Alice giggled. She remembered complaining about vegetables for breakfast when they first came to Shanghai. Now she was used to it.

"When do we go see Millie?" Grandma asked. "I'm anxious to see how she's doing."

Daddy looked down for a moment. "Um, Mom, she—she's not doing well," he finally said. "I'll take you to see her as soon as we finish breakfast. She's strongest in the morning." Daddy paused to pick up Johnny's bowl from the floor. "We can see her for only a few minutes. Her nurses will run us out. And you'll get to talk to her only from the doorway. Johnny will stay here with Poh-Poh. He wouldn't understand why he could only look at his mother."

Grandpa fussed a bit as he squeezed himself into a rickshaw with Alice.

Daddy and Grandma went in another one. At the hospital, he seemed pleased. "That's a right nice building!" he said. "When will it be finished?"

Alice put her shoulders back and felt important. "Dr. Miller says it will be finished by the end of this year," she said. "In fact, Daddy's helping him plan the big celebration on New Year's Day. Then it will be officially open. It's going to be named The Shanghai Sanitarium."

"Humph," Grandpa grunted as he climbed out. "Looks like a nice place," he said again.

Daddy led them around to a back entrance and down a short hall. He spoke quietly to a nurse sitting just outside a closed door. The nurse went into the room. A few minutes later, she opened the door.

"You may see her now," the nurse said. "But only for a few minutes. She gets tired very quickly." Then she stepped out of the doorway.

Alice held back while Grandma looked in. Grandma didn't say anything. She just reached for Grandpa's hand.

Grandpa cleared his throat and said, "We've come to see you, Millie. We'll make sure your little ones are taken care of. Don't you worry about a thing. Just get well."

Then it was Alice's turn. Daddy took her hand and stood beside her in the doorway. Alice opened her mouth to speak, but found a lump in her throat instead of words. That was Mother in the bed, she was sure of it. But her cheeks were sunk in, and she looked kind of gray.

As Alice watched, Mother raised her hand and wiggled her fingers. The smile on her face didn't quite get to both sides of her mouth.

Finally Alice blurted out, "Mother, I miss you!" As she watched, she saw a tear slide down the side of Mother's face.

When the nurse shooed them away, Daddy stood for a few minutes with his eyes shut and his hand over his mouth. Alice could see the little bump on the front of his neck going up and down. She wondered if he was trying not to cry.

Grandma didn't speak all the way home, and she blinked her eyes a lot. Once they were inside, she went straight to her bedroom. Daddy and Grandpa went into the living room and shut the door. Alice stood alone in the courtyard. Then she heard Grandpa's voice coming through the open window. She edged nearer.

Lots of Prayers

"OK, Son," she heard Grandpa say. "Tell me the truth about Millie."

"Oh, Dad! She is fading away right in front of my eyes. And I blame myself. I didn't want her to come to China, but she insisted. I should have canceled the whole idea."

"But you came because God wanted you to come. And Millie felt the same way," Grandpa said. "Right?"

"Yes," Daddy answered. "But maybe I was wrong. Maybe I just wanted to come. Maybe it wasn't God's will at all."

"You know, Son, the devil must be afraid of what you're trying to do here. He's doing his best to discourage you."

For a few minutes, neither spoke. Then Grandpa asked, "Have you had an anointing service for Millie yet?"

A PRAYER FOR MOTHER

After another pause, Daddy spoke slowly, "No, I haven't. I've prayed and pleaded with God. But I guess I needed you here to help me go further."

Alice felt a sob rising in her throat. Tears blinded her eyes. She turned and bolted toward her bedroom—and ran right into Grandma. Grandma led Alice into her bedroom and hugged her, holding her close for a moment.

When Grandma finally sat down on the bed, she pulled Alice down beside her. For a long time they just sat together, not speaking.

"Grandma?" Alice said at last. "Grandma, what's an anointing service?"

For a few seconds, Grandma didn't move. Then she asked, "Now where have you heard about that?"

"I heard Daddy and Grandpa talking about it. What is it?"

Lots of Prayers

Grandma was silent for another minute. "It's a special prayer time for a person who's very, very sick," she said. "The church pastor and other leaders of the church join together to pray—like they did in Bible times. The pastor puts a little oil on the head of the person who is ill. Then they all kneel around the person and pray for God's special healing."

Alice snuggled closer to Grandma. "And then the person gets well, right?" she asked.

"Sometimes," Grandma said sadly. "Not always. The healing must be according to God's wisdom. God knows people's hearts. And He knows the future. We don't."

"Will He heal Mother?"

"Oh, I hope so," Grandma said. "I have asked Him to—so many, many times."

A PRAYER FOR MOTHER

"But why wouldn't God heal Mother? We need her. And—and she's a missionary!"

"When we get to heaven, we'll find out why God heals some people, but not others," Grandma replied. "We won't understand it until then. But He has already answered one of my prayers."

"Really? About what?"

"Nobody else in the family is showing signs of TB," Grandma explained. "I was so concerned about that. But you and Johnny and your daddy are still healthy. And I'm so thankful."

The next day was Sabbath. Grandma and Grandpa went to church with the family. "Even if we can't understand the language," Grandpa said, "it's good to worship with God's people."

Alice sat between her grandparents. She waved to Mr. Cheng when he slid

Lots of Prayers

into an empty space beside Daddy. He came to church every Sabbath now.

Johnny sat in Daddy's lap and stared at Grandma and Grandpa.

Soon after the minister began, Alice heard a strange sound beside her. Suddenly, Grandma reached across and poked Grandpa. "You're snoring," she whispered.

Alice covered her mouth so she wouldn't giggle out loud. Then something the minister said caught her attention.

"Do you talk to God like you talk to your friends?" he asked. "Do you? Or do you just ask for things?"

Hmmm, Alice thought. *Do I do that, Jesus?*

The minister went on. "If you look at the Lord's Prayer, it begins with praise. 'Our Father in heaven, holy is

Your name.' To our friends, we might say, 'That's a nice shirt,' or 'I enjoyed the song you sang.' So why don't we find something to praise God for?"

Again, Alice paid close attention. She sat up a little straighter. Maybe if she learned how to pray just right, God would heal Mother. But . . . Grandma had said it was God's decision in the end. *Oh, please, Jesus,* she pleaded. *Please make Mother well. We need her so much.*

The minister went on. "Notice the words in the Lord's Prayer that say, 'Thy will be done on earth as it is in heaven.' What about that? When you talk to your friends, do you always demand that they do what you want?"

Alice didn't hear any more of the sermon. She was lost in her thoughts about prayer.

CHAPTER 7

"Thy Will Be Done"

"Al Lees!" Li Li called from the roof. "Can you play?"

Alice ran out of her room and looked up. "Yes, please come over."

The girls spread a mat on the concrete and sat down. Sally and her clothes were laid out. But Li Li wanted to talk.

"Al Lees, will you teach me how to pray?"

A PRAYER FOR MOTHER

Alice blinked. *Oh, dear Jesus, I don't know how to do this. Please help me!*

"Well," Alice started. "Um, first you say 'Dear Jesus,' then you just say what you want to say. Like you were talking to a friend. And you end with 'amen.' "

"Can anyone pray? Will your Jesus listen to me? Doesn't He hate Buddhists?"

"Jesus doesn't hate anyone. He created everyone, you know. He loves all people."

"You do it first," Li Li said. "Then I'll try."

Alice paused a moment, thinking about what the minister had said on Sabbath. Then she got on her knees and folded her hands.

"Dear Jesus," she prayed, "thank You for my food and clothes. And thank

"Thy Will Be Done"

You for bringing my grandma and grandpa safely to China. Please, Jesus, make Mother well soon. Amen."

When she opened her eyes, Li Li was watching her carefully. "That's all?" she asked. "You don't have to bow or burn incense to make Him happy?"

"That's all. And you don't always have to kneel. You can talk to Jesus when you walk down the street. Or when you're in school."

Li Li's eyes were open wide.

Alice smiled. "Now you try it," she said.

So the girls got on their knees side by side. They folded their hands.

After a quiet moment, Li Li began. "Dear Jesus, my name is Li Li. Thank You for my friend, Al Lees. Thank You for food. Thank You for my home. I want to belong to You like Al Lees does.

Could I? And please make Al Lees's mother well. Amen."

The girls stood up and hugged each other. "Maybe you can go to Sabbath School with me next Sabbath," Alice said.

"Could I?" Li Li's eyes were bright. "I'll ask my mother."

Just then Li Li heard her mother calling her. "I've got to go," she said. "But I'll pray again soon."

That evening after supper Daddy announced, "Tomorrow afternoon the pastor will anoint Millie. I'll come home about three and pick you up, Dad."

"Can I go too?" Alice asked.

"I'm afraid not, Little Lady. I'm sorry."

Grandma patted her arm. "You and I will have our own prayer meeting here, OK?"

"Thy Will Be Done"

It wasn't OK, but Alice knew it must be a grown-up thing, so she couldn't go.

"By the way," Grandpa said, changing the subject, "how big will this Shanghai Sanitarium be when you're finished?"

"It'll have 250 beds," Daddy said. "But only fifty of them will be for patients who can pay for hospital care."

Alice frowned. "Who gets the other beds, Daddy?"

"The other two hundred will be for charity patients—people who don't have the money for medical care."

"The people here must love Dr. Miller," Grandma said.

"They do," Daddy replied. "In fact, he's been asked several times to take a government position. But each time he tells them the same thing: 'My business is medicine, not politics.' "

A PRAYER FOR MOTHER

When Daddy and Grandpa left the next afternoon, Johnny was still taking his nap. Alice and Grandma sat in the living room, thinking about Mother.

Finally Grandma looked at the clock. "It's four o'clock," she said. "The men are starting the service for your mother right now. So let's pray, too."

They knelt close together. Grandma put her arm around Alice. Then Grandma began to pray. She thanked the Lord for His healing power. She thanked Him for Jesus' dying on the cross to save them. Then she asked Him to make Mother well and strong again. Finally, she ended her prayer with, "But even in this, Lord, Thy will be done. Amen."

Grandma's arm tightened around Alice. "Do you want to pray, too?" she asked.

"Thy Will Be Done"

Alice nodded. She began slowly. "Dear Jesus, thank You that Grandma and Grandpa are here. Thank You that Li Li wants to be a Christian." She stopped for a moment, wiped her eyes, and sniffed. "Um, Jesus? My mother is really sick. Please, please, Jesus, make her well. Johnny cries a lot for her. I need her too. And so does Daddy. So please take the TB away. Please!" she begged. Tears ran down her cheeks. She knew how she needed to end her prayer, but it was so hard to actually say the words. "Um . . . Thy will . . . be done. Amen."

For a long time, Alice sat on the sofa beside Grandma, nestled in her arms. Both wiped their tears often. They sat, lost in their thoughts, until Johnny began calling for someone to get him out of his crib.

A PRAYER FOR MOTHER

When Daddy and Grandpa came home, Mr. Cheng was with them. Alice ran to give him a big hug.

Mr. Cheng laughed. "This be a custom from America in which I have humble delight!" he said. He bowed to Grandma, and then shook her hand. "I come for the pleasure of meeting you, honored madam. And I arrange with the doctor and his honorable father to take you all to favored restaurant. You will come, yes?" He grinned at Alice. "And the little missy," he added.

They decided it was too late for Johnny, so Poh-Poh stayed with him.

At the restaurant, Alice watched Daddy talk to the others. He seemed, well, maybe not happy, but at least less sad. He and Grandpa and Mr. Cheng told stories to entertain Alice and

"Thy Will Be Done"

Grandma and to keep all their minds too busy to worry.

"Here is a happening I well remember," Mr. Cheng said, beginning another story. "It was the day Madam Stewart spoke exceedingly loud to me."

"What?" Grandpa exclaimed. "Millie? I can't imagine it!"

So Mr. Cheng told how he had often followed Alice, listening to her speak English. He told about their first meeting when Mother had faced him and demanded to know why he was following them. And how they had gone to a tea shop to talk. Alice added her own side of the story. Grandma and Grandpa laughed and laughed as they heard about it.

Mr. Cheng closed his story by saying, "Because of this, I now have good position at the new American hospital.

A PRAYER FOR MOTHER

And I have American friends. And I have learned to know God of heaven. For these things I have great thankfulness."

About a week later, Alice came out of the Miller house after school. Instead of the hospital gardener, Mr. Cheng waited for her.

"Hello, Little Missy," he said with a bow. "You honorable father asked me to bring you to the hospital."

"Why?" Alice asked. "Do you know what he wants? Is Mother OK?" Then a terrible thought struck her. *Maybe God hasn't healed Mother!*

Alice grabbed the sleeve of Mr. Cheng's long shirt. Her heart felt like it had stopped in her chest. "Is Mother dead?"

He looked startled. "Dead? No, Little One. She is asking for you!"

"Thy Will Be Done"

At the hospital, Alice held tightly to Mr. Cheng's hand as they walked down the hall together. Mother's door stood open. She heard Daddy speaking quietly inside the room. No nurse was in the hall this time.

Alice pulled back as they neared the room. What would she see? Mr. Cheng put a hand on her back to urge her forward.

"Courage, Little Missy," he said softly.

CHAPTER 8

"I Am Home"

Alice straightened her shoulders and stepped to the door. When Daddy saw her, he jumped up and led her to Mother's bed. He was smiling, but Alice didn't notice. She was staring at Mother.

Mother's skin was pink. Her eyes were bright. Her cheeks didn't even sink in anymore. Alice just stood there. Her mouth hung open. She couldn't believe her eyes.

"I *Am* Home"

Finally, Mother laughed her cheery little laugh and held her arms out to Alice.

Alice buried her face in Mother's shoulder and sobbed. Mother patted her on the back and whispered comforting words—just like she used to do.

Finally, Alice sat up and smiled through her tears. "Oh, Mother," she said, "I was afraid that you'd died!"

Mother squeezed her hand. "Not this time," she said. "God has been good to me. I am so much better that I may get to go home next week—if I promise to rest often."

Alice was too happy to speak. The wide smile that spread across her face spoke for her.

When she got home, she ran out to the courtyard and called, "Li Li! Li Li!"

A PRAYER FOR MOTHER

Li Li's head soon appeared above the living room. "Yes? What's the matter?"

"Nothing's the matter," Alice said. "But I have something important to tell you."

"What?"

"Remember when we prayed for Mother to get well?"

"Yes."

Alice couldn't keep from jumping up and down. "She's getting better! She gets to come home next week! She's not going to die! Isn't that wonderful?"

Li Li started to say something several times, but she couldn't seem to find the right words. Finally, she said, "Your God is that powerful? He really can heal people?"

Alice nodded her head up and down rapidly. "Yes, isn't it great? It's a miracle!"

"I *Am* Home"

That evening, the grown-ups talked about living arrangements in the house.

"Millie will need to be in her own bed," Grandma said. "But she'll need our help, so we shouldn't go home just yet. Should we move to an inn?"

"Definitely not," Daddy said firmly. "I've been thinking about this. I think the living-room furniture will fit in one end of the dining room. Then we'll turn the living room into your bedroom. I'll get a bed delivered before Millie comes home."

"If you're OK with that, Son," Grandpa said, "it will work for us."

A month after Mother came home, she was much better. But she was still weak. She didn't even have enough strength to lift Johnny. So one Sunday afternoon, Daddy called a family meeting. Johnny played under the table with a small truck Grandpa had brought him. The rest of the family sat around the table, eager to hear what Daddy wanted to discuss with them.

Daddy first prayed for God to give them wisdom. Then he said, "I think we should talk about our future. Mom and Dad, I wanted you in on this too since it could involve you. The big question for me is about Millie."

Mother looked up quickly. "What about me? I'm well, really I am."

"But you're not strong yet." Daddy ran his hands through his hair. "I'm thinking you and the children should go back to America when my parents go." He looked at Grandpa. "They could live with you, Dad, couldn't they? Until I can leave here? I'd need to stay until they found another doctor to take my place."

"I *Am* Home"

Daddy looked around at all the silent faces. Finally Grandpa spoke.

"Of course they'd be welcome on the farm, but is that really what you want?"

"Millie needs to be in the country for a while," Daddy said. "Dr. Miller said I should take her somewhere where it's cooler. Somewhere where the air is clean."

"Yes, but you're talking about going back to America for good, aren't you, Son?"

"Yes." Daddy looked down at his hands. Then he raised his head and spoke. "These months of Millie's illness have been terrible for all of us. I don't want to go through that again. I think we should go home."

"But, John," Mother said, "I could have caught TB in Portland, too. And I had the best possible doctor's care right

91

here. And good nursing care, too. And don't forget that God healed me. Did He do that so we could run away?"

Daddy looked surprised and stared at her. "You mean," he said, "that after all you've been through, you still want to stay in China?"

"Don't you?" Mother asked. "Didn't we believe we were doing what God wanted us to when we came here?"

Alice's mind wandered while the family talked about going or staying. Did she really want to go back to America right now? Did she want to leave Li Li and Mr. Cheng? And Poh-Poh? And the Sabbath Schools she prepared for the neighborhood children? Grocery stores would seem boring after going to the market in Shanghai. And she rather liked going to a home-school with only a few other students.

"I *Am* Home"

"Alice?" Daddy said, touching her hand. "Are you still with us?"

Alice felt her face turning hot. "Yes, Daddy."

"What do you think about us going home?" he asked.

Alice paused a moment. Then an amazing thought popped into her mind.

"But, Daddy," she said, "I *am* home."

The grown-ups all stared at her. Mother brushed a tear from her eye. Finally Grandma said, "Bless the child!"

Grandpa's voice was husky when he spoke. "Here's another idea," he said. "Is there somewhere here in China where you could vacation for a month or so? Maybe somewhere up in the mountains south of Shanghai? It would be cooler, and the air would be nice and fresh."

A PRAYER FOR MOTHER

Daddy stroked his chin. "I've heard other missionaries talk about going to the mountains. I could check on that." He looked at Mother. "How does that sound, Millie?"

"By all means, see what you can find out," she answered. "Maybe we can rent a bungalow big enough for all of us. It would be fun!"

"Dad? Mom? Can you stay here for a while and go with us? We could use your help."

Grandpa nodded. "I'm a retired farmer now, so I don't have to get back in time for harvest. We could stay for a bit longer. See what you can find out."

Mother smiled. "The Lord has taken care of us so far. He'll help us find just the right place if—" she looked at Grandpa with a grin "—if you're brave enough to eat the food in another part of China!"

Grandpa patted his round stomach. "I'm not starving so far, am I? Besides, I'll bring a fork."

They all laughed.

"OK," Daddy said. "I'll find a place up in the mountains where we can enjoy a month of holiday." Daddy looked at each face. "Millie will get strong again. And I'll have my first break from work since we came here. Then we'll come back to work for God in Shanghai." He looked at Alice with a warm smile. "We'll come back home."

Thank You, Jesus, Alice prayed silently. *Thank You for healing Mother. Thank You for my home. And thank You for letting me be a missionary.*

If you liked meeting Alice, you've got to meet Sarah, Elizabeth, and Heather—the other Adventist girls!

Sarah, An Adventist Girl (Set 1)

By *Jean Boonstra*. These stories are about a young pioneer girl named Sarah Barnes living in the days of William Miller between 1842 and 1844. This four-book series will entertain and educate children about their Adventist heritage and hope. Titles are: 1. *A Song for Grandfather*; 2. *Miss Button and the School Board*; 3. *A secret in the Family*; 4. *Sarah's Disappointment*.

0-8163-1907-3. Paperback. US$24.99, Can$37.49 set.

Elizabeth, An Adventist Girl, (Set 2)

By *Kay D. Rizzo*. One day, two mystery guests from Maine arrive at Elizabeth's house. The woman, Mrs. White, has visions from God. Big changes happen in Elizabeth's family. Titles are: 1. *The Not-So-Secret Mission*; 2. *Old Friends and New*; 3. *Bells and Whistles*; 4. *Wagon Train West*.

4-33300311-3. Paperback. US$24.99, Can$37.49 set.

Heather, An Adventist Girl (Set 3)

By *Jean Boonstra*. The year is 1898. Heather Gibson can hardly believe her family is moving to Australia. This was the time when Ellen White lived there and wrote her beautiful books on the life of Christ. Meet the new friends and visit the amazing places that become part of Heather's world, in these fun-to-read stories. Titles are: 1. *Secrets and Friends*; 2. *A New Life Down Under*; 3. *A Wedding in Avondale*; 4. *Going Home*.

4-3330-0336-6. Paperback. US$24.99, Can$37.49 set.

Each episode in the Adventist Girl historical series will entertain and educate children about the Adventist heritage and hope.

Order from your ABC by calling **1-800-765-6955**, or get online and shop our virtual store at **www.AdventistBookCenter.com**.
- Read a chapter from your favorite book
- Order online
- Sign up for email notices on new products